HAPPY BIRTHDAY!

My name is _____.

I was born on _____, _____.
                  (day of the week)   (month, day, and year)

I was born at _____.
                      (hour, minute, A.M. or P.M.)

I was born in _____,
                   (city, state, country)

  at _____.
             (place)

I weighed _____.

I measured _____ long.

I was born with _____ hair
               (color)
  and _____ eyes.
         (color)

I was born with _____ hair.
          (hardly any, a little bit of, lots of)

THANK YOU TO THE BABIES AND PARENTS—
Ben, David and Bill, Samuel and Mona, Emma, Sam, Karen, and Bill

~

THANK YOU TO THE BABY DOCTORS—
Merton Bernfield, Sarah Birss, T. Berry Brazelton, Peter Gorski, Gerry Hass, Penelope Leach,
Laura Riley, Ralph Ross, Barry Zuckerman, and Pamela Zuckerman

~

THANK YOU TO THE BABY NURSES—
Mary Ellen Flanagan and Amy Steele-Bucci

~

A special thank you to Lindsey Rae, Trish, and Ray

Text copyright © 1996 by Robie H. Harris
Illustrations copyright © 1996 by Michael Emberley

First paperback edition 2002

The Library of Congress has cataloged the hardcover edition as follows:

Harris, Robie H.
Happy birth day! / by Robie H. Harris : illustrated by Michael Emberley. —1st ed.
p.   cm.
Summary: A mother tells her child about its first day of life from the
moment of birth through the end of the birth day.
ISBN 1-56402-424-5 (hardcover)
[1. Childbirth—Fiction. 2. Babies—Fiction.]   I. Emberley, Michael, ill.   II. Title.
PZ7.H2436Hap   1996
[E]—dc20   95-34547

ISBN 0-7636-0974-9 (paperback)

2 4 6 8 10 9 7 5 3

Printed in Hong Kong

This book was typeset in Palatino.
The illustrations were done in pencil and pastel.

Candlewick Press
2067 Massachusetts Avenue
Cambridge, Massachusetts 02140

visit us at www.candlewick.com

HAPPY BIRTH DAY!

by
Robie H. Harris

illustrated by
Michael Emberley

CANDLEWICK PRESS
CAMBRIDGE, MASSACHUSETTS

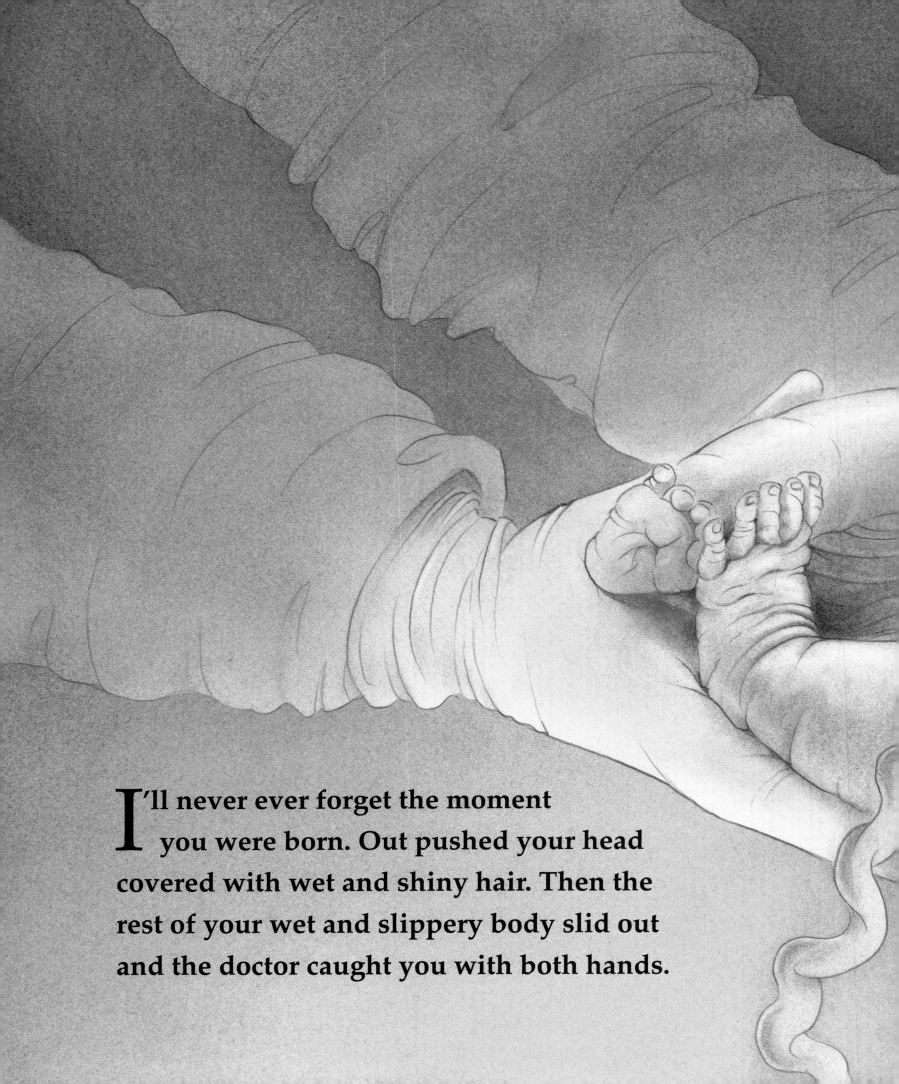

I'll never ever forget the moment
you were born. Out pushed your head
covered with wet and shiny hair. Then the
rest of your wet and slippery body slid out
and the doctor caught you with both hands.

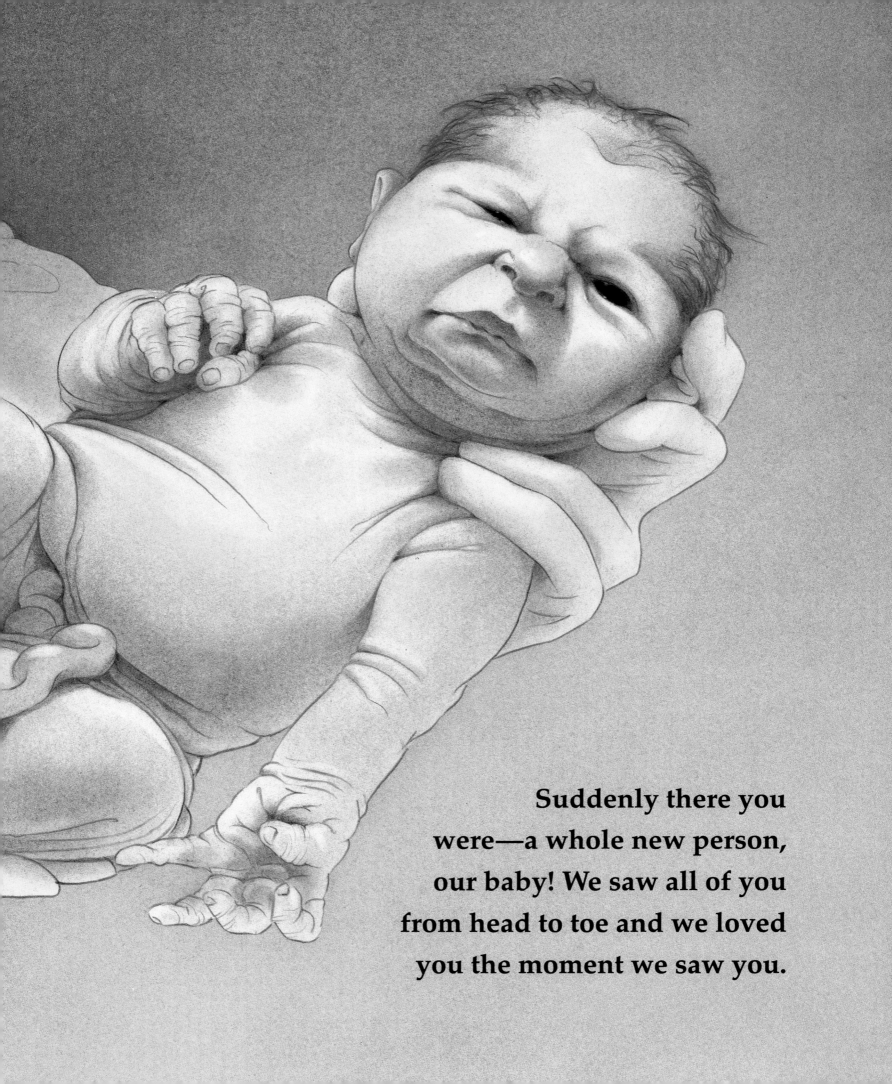

Suddenly there you
were—a whole new person,
our baby! We saw all of you
from head to toe and we loved
you the moment we saw you.

You let out a loud cry—about as loud as a coyote howling at the moon. It was hard to believe that someone so tiny and new in the world could cry so loud. But you did.

Your cry filled your lungs with air and you took your very first breath. Even though you were only a few seconds old, you were breathing on your own.

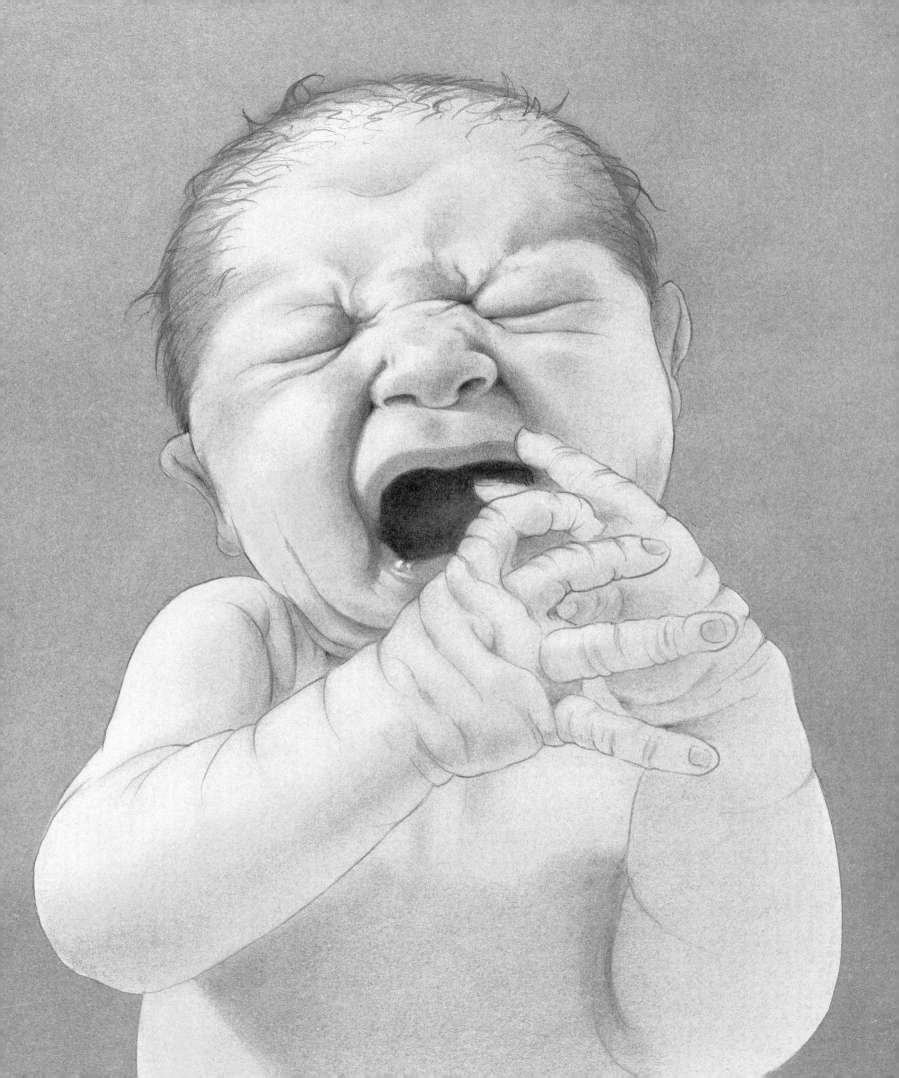

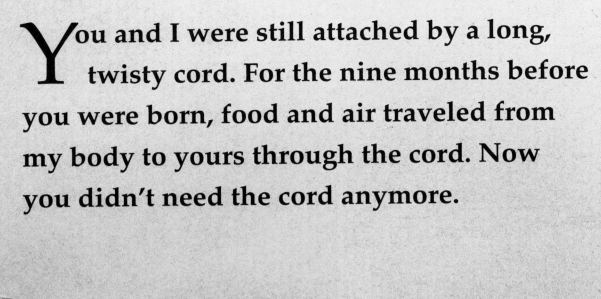

You and I were still attached by a long, twisty cord. For the nine months before you were born, food and air traveled from my body to yours through the cord. Now you didn't need the cord anymore.

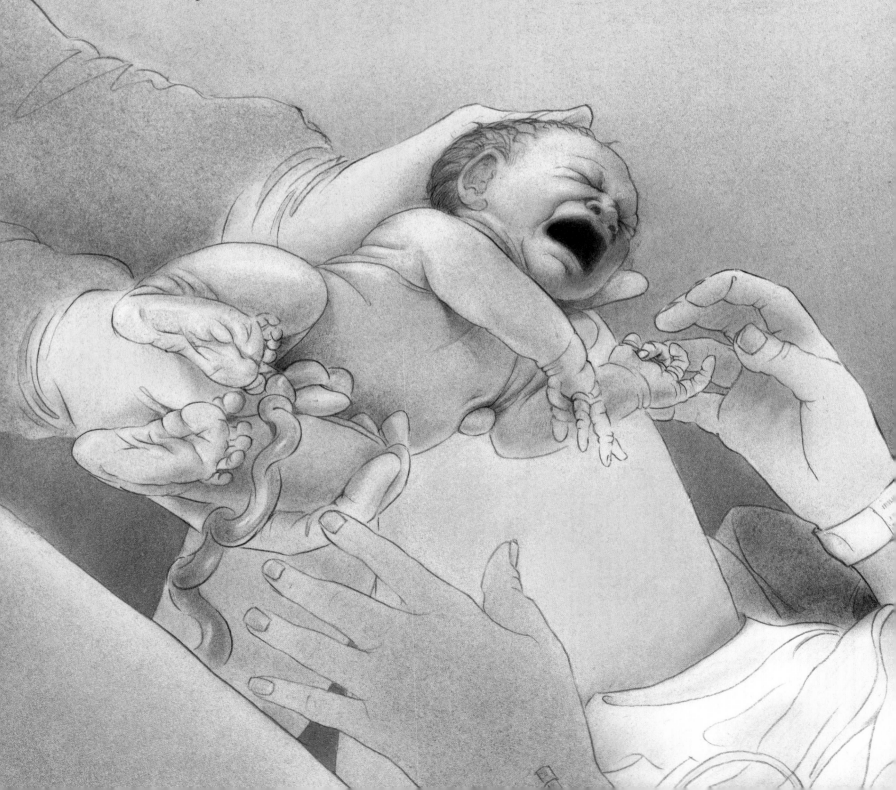

So the doctor quickly put a clamp on it and snipped it. Thank goodness neither you nor I could feel the snip! It didn't hurt at all. I reached for you, and the doctor laid you in my arms.

I was so happy to finally hold you! Your breath on my cheek felt as warm as toast and your skin against mine felt as soft as wrinkled velvet.

Daddy kissed the top of your head and I kissed your cheek. Then the nurse quickly covered you with a blanket and slipped a hat on your head to keep you warm and dry. Your eyes opened slowly and you gazed at me for a long time.

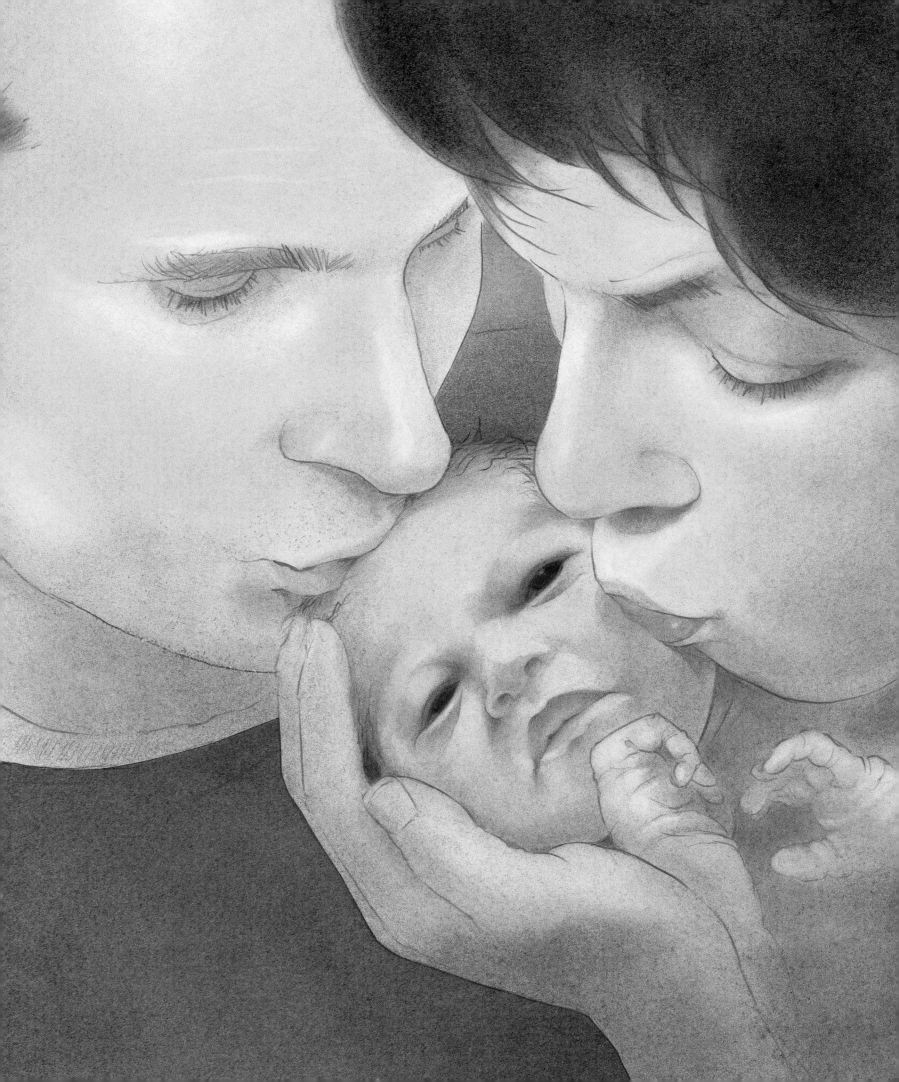

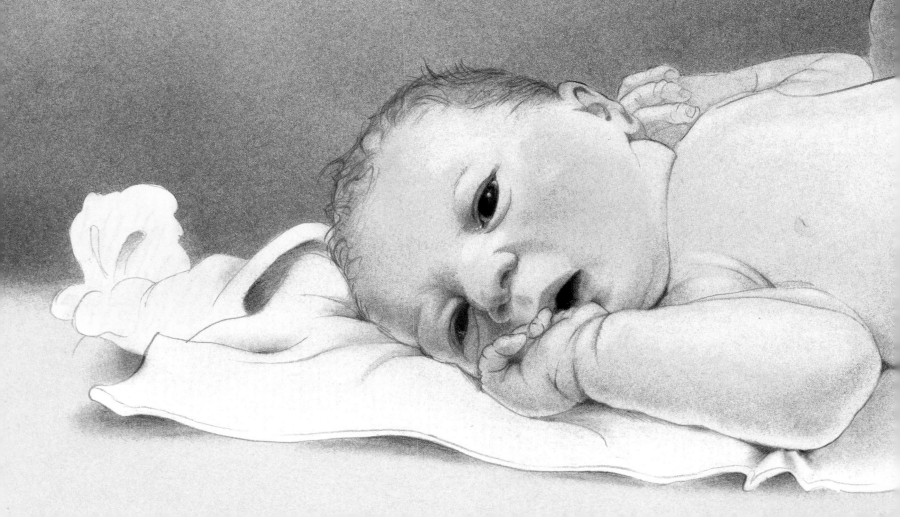

Moments later, the doctor took a good look at you and told us how healthy and how beautiful you were.

The nurse put bracelets with our family name around your ankles so that everyone would know you were our baby. Then she quickly weighed and measured you, sponged you off and dried you, and wrapped you up again. You stayed wide awake the whole time!

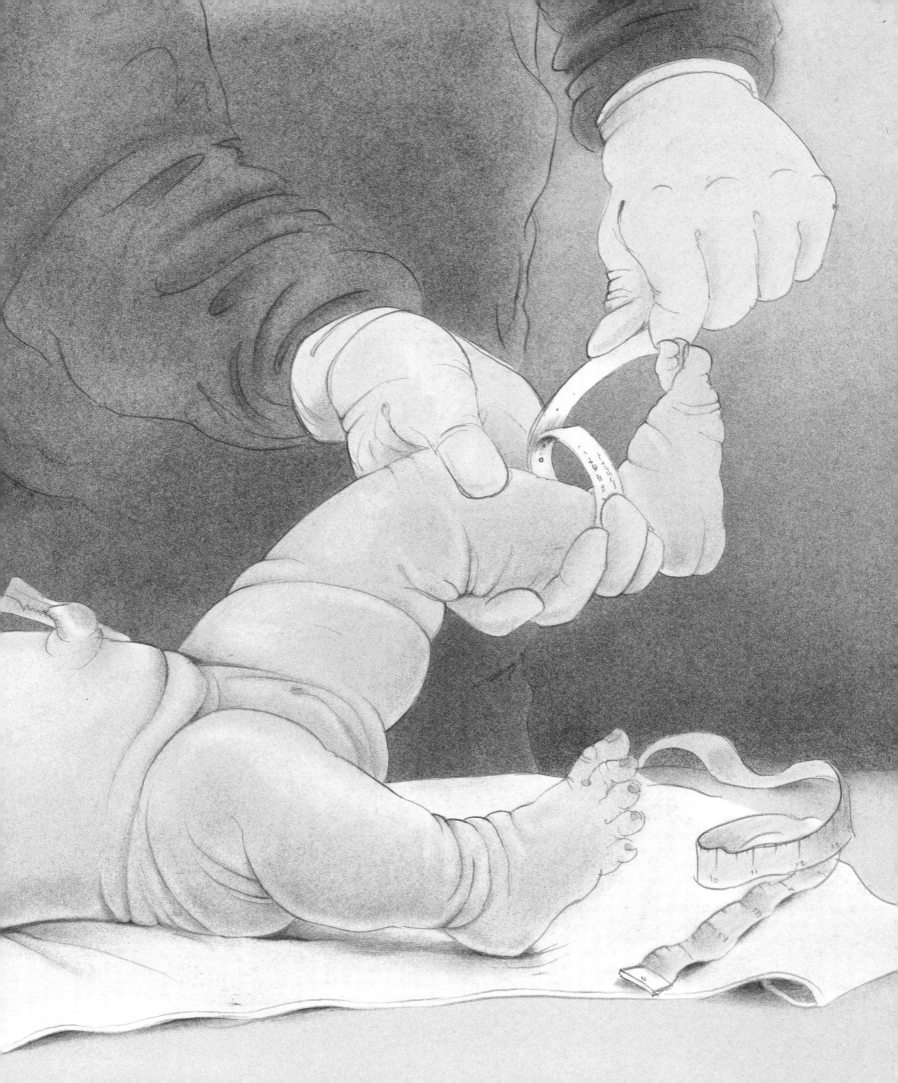

Daddy scooped you up like a football and held you tight. You looked so cozy and peaceful all bundled up in Daddy's arms. Your thumb slid into your mouth and you sucked on it. And soon your eyes began to close.

Being born must have been very hard work—seeing light, hearing new sounds, feeling air on your skin, and just being brand-new in the world. No wonder you were tired.

While you slept, our best friends walked in with a furry stuffed bear for you. Your great-aunt wheeled in a bright red tricycle. Your cousin brought you a drawing of her dog. And your uncle couldn't stop snapping pictures of you.

Everyone was so happy and so excited to finally meet you!

You began to whimper, and suddenly you were awake. I picked you up and you snuggled into my shoulder. But then your lips began to quiver and you opened your mouth and cried. I thought you might never stop!

But as I gently stroked your cheek, you took a big deep breath—and stopped. Then you squiggled up your nose and began to nurse. You made such sweet smacking sounds! Daddy said you sounded like a baby goat.

After you nursed, I held you over my shoulder and rubbed your back. You burped. It was a loud one! Soon after that, you peed and pooped. Daddy changed your diaper and you sneezed twice. Then, you began to hiccup.

All that noise made us laugh. We were amazed that someone so little could make so many noises and do so many things at once. Finally, you yawned and fell asleep again—and it was so quiet.

That evening, Grandma and Grandpa came to meet you. They talked to you about all the splendid things you and they would do together—go to the movies, eat ice cream, make snow angels, paint pictures, bake cookies, catch fish, build sandcastles, ride bikes, and fly kites.

Even though you were less than one day old, they loved talking to you.

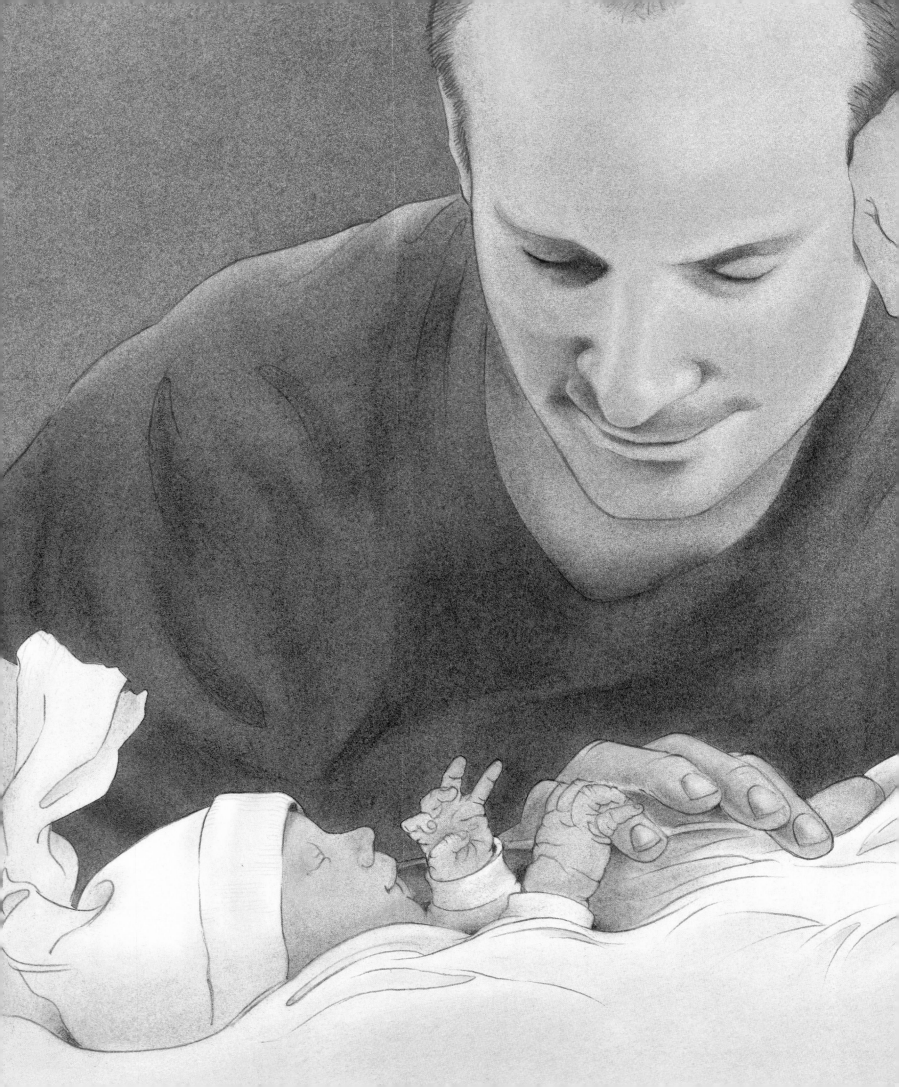

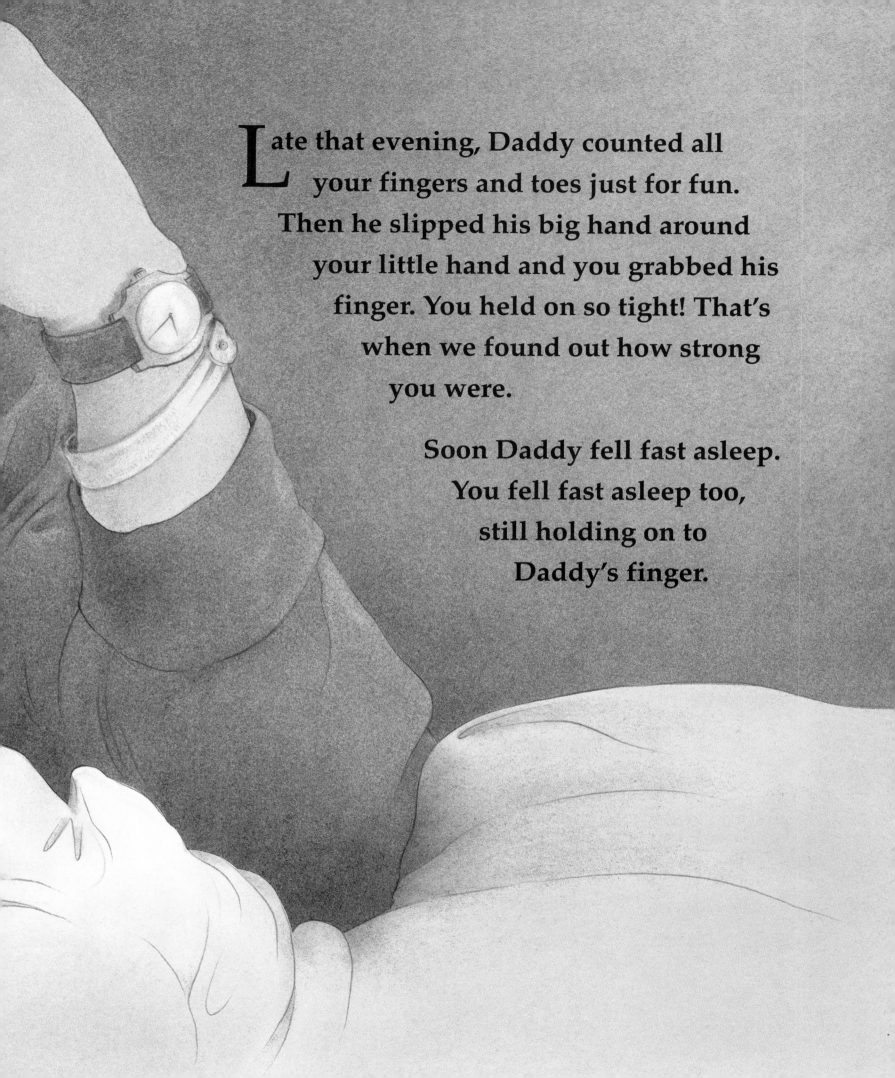

Late that evening, Daddy counted all
your fingers and toes just for fun.
Then he slipped his big hand around
your little hand and you grabbed his
finger. You held on so tight! That's
when we found out how strong
you were.

Soon Daddy fell fast asleep.
You fell fast asleep too,
still holding on to
Daddy's finger.

I looked at you snuggled in between Daddy and me and I kissed you both good night. You were only a day old, but you didn't seem so new anymore. I felt as if I had known you forever.

"Happy Birth Day!" I whispered to you, and soon I fell fast asleep too.

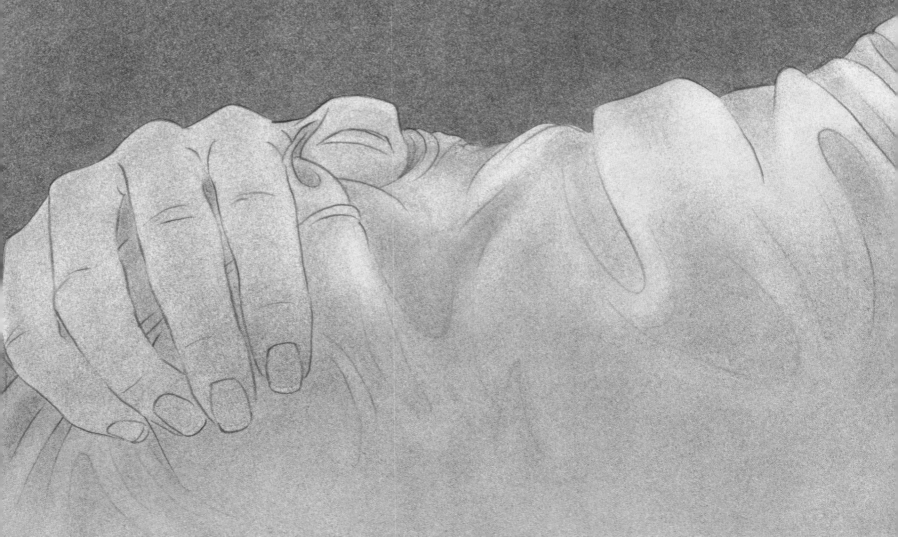